P
Noah

"Dense, clever, and unpr[...] [...]e-
quences that bend and twist toward a visionary apocalypse,
whose music levitates the form and presents new ways of
reading it." —Ray González, *The Bloomsbury Review*

"Deftly maneuvers links of language from theory to litera-
ture, to love." —Jane Sprague, *Boog City*

"Splendid and varied." —Culture Industry

"At times insanely surreal." —Jacket

"Gestures of resistance to hegemony in Gordon's work uti-
lize parody, flirt with aphorism, but richly refuse simple pre-
scription." —Thomas Fink, Octopus

"Cascades of images and precisely tumbling syntax.... A
hallowed new world flush in art and music."
  —*Publishers Weekly*

"Rich and compelling." —*Rain Taxi*

"This book *revs up the infinite*."
  —*Sentence: A Journal of Prose Poetics*

"Virtuoso display of sound and meaning."
  —Luke Kennard, *Stride* magazine

"A Dionysian appreciation, even wonder, at the physical ma-
teriality and mystery of words." —Rusty Morrison, *Traffic*

"Musical and literary." —*Xantippe*

Joshua Marie Wilkinson

About the Author

NOAH ELI GORDON is the author of *A Fiddle Pulled from the Throat of a Sparrow* (New Issues, 2007), *Figures for a Darkroom Voice* (in collaboration with Joshua Marie Wilkinson, Tarpaulin Sky, 2007), *Inbox* (BlazeVOX, 2006), *The Area of Sound Called the Subtone* (Ahsahta Press, 2004), and *The Frequencies* (Tougher Disguises, 2003), as well as numerous chapbooks, including *That We Come to a Consensus* (in collaboration with Sara Veglahn, Ugly Duckling Presse, 2005). He teaches at the University of Colorado at Denver.

NOVEL
PICTORIAL
NOISE

Also by Noah Eli Gordon

BOOKS

The Frequencies (2003)

The Area of Sound Called the Subtone (2004)

Inbox (2006)

A Fiddle Pulled from the Throat of a Sparrow (2007)

Figures for a Darkroom Voice (2007; with Joshua Marie Wilkinson)

CHAPBOOKS AND LIMITED EDITION PAMPHLETS

The Fire and the Blue (2002; with Nick Moudry)

Ten Frequencies (2002)

A Falling in Autumn (2003; with Peter Gregorio)

The Laughing Alphabet (2004)

Untitled (Whalebone) Essays (2004; with Eric Baus, Nick Moudry, and Travis Nichols)

Notes Toward the Spectacle (2004)

Jaywalking the Is (2004)

What Ever Belong in the Circle (2004)

How Human Nouns (2004)

That We Come to a Consensus (2005; with Sara Veglahn)

Twenty Ruptured Paragraphs from a Perfectly Functional Book (2006)

A New Hymn to the Old Night (2006; split release with Michael Friedman)

Flag (2006)

The National Poetry Series was established in 1978 to ensure the publication of five poetry books annually through participating publishers. Publication is funded by the Lannan Foundation; the late James A. Michener and Edward J. Piszek through the Copernicus Society of America; Stephen Graham; International Institute of Modern Letters; Joyce and Seward Johnson Foundation; Juliet Lea Hillman Simonds Foundation; and the Tiny Tiger Foundation. This project also is supported in part by an award from the National Endowment for the Arts, which believes that a great nation deserves great art.

2006 Open Competition Winners

Laynie Browne of Oakland, California, *The Scented Fox*
Chosen by Alice Notley, to be published by Wave Books

Noah Eli Gordon of Denver, Colorado, *Novel Pictorial Noise*
Chosen by John Ashbery, to be published by Harper Perennial

Laurie Clements Lambeth of Houston, Texas, *Veil and Burn*
Chosen by Maxine Kumin, to be published by University of Illinois Press

Martha Ronk of Los Angeles, California, *Vertigo*
Chosen by C. D. Wright, to be published by Coffee House Press

William Stobb of La Crosse, Wisconsin, *Nervous Systems*
Chosen by August Kleinzahler, to be published by Penguin Books

NOVEL

PICTORIAL

NOISE

Noah Eli Gordon

HARPER  PERENNIAL

NEW YORK • LONDON • TORONTO • SYDNEY

HARPER ● PERENNIAL

NATIONAL
ENDOWMENT
FOR THE ARTS

HarperCollins books may be purchased for educational, business, or sales promotional use. For information please write: Special Markets Department, HarperCollins Publishers, 10 East 53rd Street, New York, NY 10022.

FIRST EDITION

Designed by Justin Dodd

Library of Congress Cataloging-in-Publication Data
Gordon, Noah Eli.
Novel pictorial noise / Noah Eli Gordon.—1st Harper Perennial ed.
p. cm.—(The national poetry series)

ISBN: 978-0-06-125703-2
ISBN-10: 0-06-125703-6

07 08 09 10 11 ID/RRD 10 9 8 7 6 5 4 3 2 1

For Michael Labenz and Juliana Leslie

Acknowledgments

Thanks to the following editors for including paragraphs from this book in their journals: S. Burgess, Amber Nelson, and Will Gallien at *Alice Blue Review*; Matthew and Katy Henriksen at *Cannibal*; Steven D. Schroeder at *The Eleventh Muse*; Ken Rumble, Tony Tost, and Chris Vitiello at *Fascicle*; Jon Thompson at *Free Verse*; Nathaniel Mackey at *Hambone*; Dennis Phillips, Martha Ronk, Standard Schaefer, and Paul Vangelisti at *The New Review of Literature*; Chad Sweeney and David Holler at *Parthenon West*; Daniel Bouchard at *The Poker*; Michael Friedman at *Shiny*; and Robert Lopez and Derek White at *Sleeping Fish*. Thanks to Peter Ganick for publishing an earlier version of portions of this manuscript in the chapbook *twenty ruptured paragraphs from a perfectly functional book*. Seven of these paragraphs were written during the first few days of January 2005; the rest were composed between May and December 2005.

The world is clanking: noun, noun, noun.

—ELIZABETH WILLIS

so silence is pictorial
when silence is real

—BARBARA GUEST

NOVEL
PICTORIAL
NOISE

COMES A night-light's landing beacon leads me to pick villainy from a bouquet of the places I'd left to yesterday's map of the future, rubber-necking unintentionally oblique articulation. Loosen a rivet from the lapsed mind and out pours the obvious like thick rain. A sterile neighborhood, a standing ovation, centuries of labor congealing into the desk lamp that lets me mold my own two cents from this paper-clip panopticon. I'm not pushing anything here. Power's got a fulcrum that's half self-portrait, part handicraft. The lever will pivot regardless of where it's placed down. It's the primacy of motion drafts sound.

composition of noise A thought is music is

    concept

STRIKING AN ORACULAR NOTE to flush out the lazy assumptions lodged within one's skull won't offer comment on some recurrent aspect of life, as the world's not weirder than we think, but weirder than we *can* think. For example, a yellow moth appears to pass through a blue tire in the painting above my understanding of geometry. The question arises: is this a picture of the distance between yellow and blue, or is it merely a means to ground the figures, a maxim bled of its proverbial exigencies, such that the only relevant plane remaining is constituted entirely by the hue of the grass—the ground over which anyone wishing to approach must pass.

between What draws
equates of

•

4

•

SOMEWHERE, a garage door goes down. Thus, a fiction begins. Clouds gather, disperse. Let this suffice as a working formula for working a formula: what I'm coming to terms with—repetition's liberating constraint. What occurs in the courtly world has little currency to those taking up arms against it. What I'm coming to terms with builds that which contains the components to construct an evolving sense of entropy. The grand narrative the end of narratives had had had had no grandiose ending. It is as though in removing its mask the landscape shows on its face an expression one recognizes but is unable to immediately place.

as through
between
definitive

6

WHEN THE ACTUAL IS transformed into its representation, representation becomes actualized, as though a net were cast not to catch whatever punctures its vicinity, but to make transparent the lapse of possession one proffers through the introduction, disappearance, and reappearance of an image whose architecture is such that in setting forth one is simultaneously building a synonym for backtracking, a barrier torn down, erected again in a slightly more ominous manner, the knowledge of instability orbiting, uncertain where to land, until one realizes that every action contains a kind of flag waving, a constituency worthy of saving.

implicit center

a cricket first

•

8

•

Not to exhibit a certain lack of clarity as to what belongs to what, but why pay homage to a postcard view from the Mount of Purgatory when it's uselessness that gives the awareness you're trying to occasion its objectionably opaque horizon? A representative tree or a representation of the tree's substitution. This business of making pictures rapidly becomes a burden. One desires to strip from the tool its use value, fulfilling the promise of cinema with the flickering image of a projector's endless rotation. As in its cutting, so in its details. What example doesn't contain the blooming topography of its own terminology?

purpose is to Cloud marks

CULTIVATING LOOSENESS is one way to proceed in the arts. A standard yard yields a sense of ownership. This is a metaphor in which grass grows lionlike in stature, in which a lion fails to garner its inauspicious standing. Coasting on the accomplishments of one's DNA demands an insurmountable allegiance to the awe an electrical socket inspires. In this way, a vehicle moves the ground beneath it. A view is merely disregard for the remaining senses. The jury's still out on nobility, though there's a tiny crown for whoever makes the loudest sound.

a frame elicits The afternoon from an example,
object

•

•

THAT IT IS NO LONGER NECESSARY to know much of anything is the noisy irony of the information age. A leaf meets its shadow on concrete to show that falling is from the council of interior constructs. Thus, the classic problem of picture book theory. Einstein called arbitrariness the greatest blunder of his life. If a branch brings to the window the image of an entire oak, then the law of accelerating returns enacts its counterexample through a model forest in a mock-up diorama of density's practical applications. Order is undoubtedly information that fits a purpose, whether expressed in ones and zeros or colored in crayon by someone imitating a child's hand.

of their Pictures a present view

THE ESSENCE of pictorial fact aspires to describe itself as a panorama, an impossible cultivation of pictorial elements. I hold that thinking is an image of art. Therefore, in proposing the helicopter as the only subject retaining any seriousness, one is concurrently giving rise to the fundamental ineptness of abstraction. For example, suppose I see an aesthetic accident rather than the intension expounded in the translator's preface. Might we then say that the architecture of the gallery space is an analogy for the plasticity of the figurative? The neutrality of such a proof is no more erroneous than the landing pad one might position on one's roof.

lost acting for measure for expression for
avoidance

I T'S ENOUGH to know something so indefensibly
small one registers it as the irritating trace of
a thought—a far-off sound, or symptom one is
unable to account for—rather than its passage into
a palpable, tactile present, or accrual into the dis-
ease one felt was there all along, waiting to surface
in the way a sudden lack of music, its intensely
abrupt rest, signals to one that yes, there was a
song in the background, you were listening to it,
and, although it was pleasant, it was nothing other
than an organized distraction, allowing you to bet-
ter concentrate on the real task at hand, turning
smallness into something grand.

then a poem like listening okay in order

I F YOU SEE the straight highway before you is permanently closed, then a picture is conjured to fix ambiguity. Although a rope doesn't ask for its knot, any expression is merely detour dressed with intention, a side road muddied from constant use. Why should a thread understand a carpet? Unimportant that my arrows point anywhere, accidental that an actual wind moves them. As always, this road ends behind us. Why should a machine be anything other than a picture of itself, when meaning and purpose read as vestments of design and one has the burden of officiating doubt on one's mind?

and so

as vocal

with which

one had

toward definition

of a kind

PIPE DREAMING your way to plasticity, to arti-
ficial light in an indoor forest, vegetable oil
growing from trees, giving the enzymes their own
private engines. It's the insect an inch from my face
convinces me design can't drive the human mind.
How else corrupt one's mother wit with prenatal
beauty? Bless the beasts for all things unawares.
Clothing's to cover a body as skin's to reveal it. In
some cases it's about faces, the opposite's true. Cir-
cular logic shaping an idea one can walk through.

now a change or more

these

Where there is

•

•

WELCOME THE INTRACTABLE AIR in which ideas are executed. Best to ignore the warning signs. Sun glints off a guillotine as easily as a gardenia eats it. I'm going to do what I'm going to do, a marker of the future tense giving off noxious fumes. This kind of choreography makes me ache all over. First, they ask for the handful of notes hovering in the background of a neo-Faustian ascent to coalesce into the bugle call an army's after. Next, the Dictionary of Cultural Literacy's completely blank. Make of my work an acrimonious analogy to an instruction manual if you must, I simply denote the encroachment of rust.

prior

listen

a note, a perfect thing

•

•

THE PROBLEM of doing justice to sun coming over the hills, morning light accentuating dust on a bureau's surface, then becoming the surface, as one collects the vagrant thoughts of last night's proposition for tomorrow into a tenuous plan for today's action, a course to be followed for its familiarity, for the comfort of greeting again that particular tree, trinkets arranged on a neighbor's lawn, the same attempt to decode graffiti on the back of a stop sign, rather than the difficulty of inundating one's self in an alien landscape, which, with its stultifying complexity of surplus imagery, forces one to simultaneously recognize and reject textual symmetry.

●

●

here This surface its presence
One both There in that

It's what's behind me keeps the carrot out front. Nostalgia printed on a new T-shirt or an old theater prop painted to match the shifty mood rings junk-drawered a decade ago. Time curls round the bend. Furls round the end? Girls in the glen? You can see them make chase below, giving the balloon another infusion of the hot air such a vantage point's full of. Wonder if death by falling sandbag's any worse than having to trim all the grass in this valley with such dull scissors. I'd slip Sisyphus into the metaphor if it weren't so flat. One does something over for the sake of getting it better. Two do something under the weather.

you of an other line Extend one onto an otherwise

BEGINNER'S REGURGITATION? Now there's a blockbox to let the pen shrivel in. Pass me those garrulous aside mongers wheat-pasting this uniform penitence over every wall the city will spare. A nail fastens. A grievance brigade points to its fingerprints on all the lists outliving us, complaint department come-ons seeping through the cleanup crew. Is there a vestige of the Velcro wars worth its place on the mantel? So what a line's potentially infinite. The globe may be the worst object ever invented. It comes down to marketing. It goes up to management. It takes more ink than you might think.

it's this force lacks an out of out

ENOUGH Polonius already. Time passes fashionably in this garden's frozen discard pile. The world and its edges aligned. Who needs the vertical effects of harmony? It's silent music moves its way through threaded integers of a luxurious capsizing, a loose-knit caller holding on the complaint line. Noise requires less effort on the part of the players. One thing clangs. A second shifts through. Next, unencumbered notes are chipped off the rising brass, hung in fish air, a harvest of digest condensation loaded onto one's questioning of the criteria for such an experience. Litigating daylight'll suffice, ignoring ubiquity's call for advice.

melody, nameless
history, as well

as well as

WOULD YOU CHOOSE the event or the box from which it's broadcast? A shadow mars the screen. Light blinds the owl. The enemy of the sunflower is perfectly still. Thus we arrive at the problem of departure. Perfect stillness requires dexterous melodrama. By definition, actors are interchangeable. A shadow mars the screen now that the night sky has dislodged a light snow. I think of the hunt I've no dog in, invert the thought to return an heirloom of excess conjecture to the auctioneer's kennel. The owl is asleep. The sunflower is asleep. Dogs are sleeping. Snow falls over my perpetual excuse, turning the narrative loose.

a storybook

clouds Time

Clouds prose

•

•

A PHOTOGRAPH. A photograph admits. A photograph admits space. A photograph admits space around its subject. A photograph admits space around its subject's a way to feel contained. I admit contentment with the Ajax bottle above the sink Alice Neel made from oils. I admit a train whistle, a dab of wisteria, a strip of duct tape's upturned corner. Coincidental nonchalance or comic fortitude? I admit both, admitting this sort of disposition harbors dangerous potential. Cue the music and evening's wash of unaccomplishment meant to make amends with whatever the day left undone does it. Now, I'm admitting a hue of a bluish green, adding color to the scene.

a building plays into explanation

as it appears to illustrate without

A GOOD ILLUSTRATION's the role of analogy. How plainly can I put this when I'm prone to revealing the totality of abstract representation shredding some few photographs of an innocuous pile of leaves brought to the picture of autumn I was after? Migratory condensation standing in for the marvelous. Pristine prehistory for an unfolded arson report. Snow over pine trees needs no corollary. I waste an afternoon dismantling the paradox it took all morning to make. Were it not possible to work out a system for one's self from the details a day's cloistered around, that potted geranium hanging above the porch wouldn't be a part of the quiet mess with which we're interminably blessed.

sound of a thought explaining

ALREADY the metaphors seem stale, having stalled in their attempt to carry us over, attention drawn to axle instead of wheel, hinge instead of door, to the slope of an animal's vertebrae over the phylum under which it's calcified, cracked into place, in essence, a privileging of anonymity, of unlikeness as a focal point, as though a bridge were to appear suddenly before us, crossing neither treacherous body of water nor maze of roadway, simply offering one another way of going on, an obligatory amazement with the plentitude of defenses guarding all of our senses.

into one admission into one idea
a crowd is experience

SUPPOSE IT WERE TRUE that one subtracts from nothing a liminal sort of freedom, as though called upon to render a wordless description of the barbed shadow an evergreen casts over figures locked in a photograph, one were to simply amplify the order, extract from the tree its treeness, adjudication from the camera, from the image its latency, logic from logic, displacing too much water and sinking the raft. Earth moves its pronouns everywhere. All beautiful dancers are boring. A red smudge on a red sky is radically corrigible. To annul a model of the universe one need only assemble it in reverse.

holds thought The space

an order to affirm context

•

•

TWO LETTERS LIE on the white tabletop: one personal and one impersonal. The desire to create a space in which one might avoid both romantic posturing and ironic detachment. No matter how often I click on this icon, the beetle refuses to come out of its box. An exercise in ambivalence. Forgive me for falling back on a doctrine which is foundational. An image accentuates the noun from which it emanates. Two letters lie on a white tabletop: one personal and one impersonal. In order to avoid shipwreck, a vessel must head into the storm. Let these examples suffice; two letters on a table generating an imperceptible fable.

through of that which gives This sort of hope its
scrutiny in what is

SHALL WE ALLOW THE QUESTION of what con-
stitutes a speaking subject to answer itself?
I'm attempting to be inclusive here. A camera
pans from left to right, appears to reorient a fig-
ure absent from the frame, renders a flexibly
combative abdication from the photograph of a
castle drawn in crayon. This is what we might call
a process. Reach the end of the board and you're
allotted a higher notch on the whipping post of a
ghost hierarchy's boldfaced blacklist. This is what
we might call the cost of capital equipment. As a
mechanical delivery system fails to account for the
weight of another clause scratched onto its sur-
face, so I attempt via the unknown to give gram-
mar a purpose.

is to
to the
on which
does not
for the

is this a picture

PRIVILEGE EXACTNESS AND PRECISION or appropriate the divine individual sucker punched by superlatives? Here indecision's doomed me for the umpteenth, its gale winds working the teapot toward pious clarity. Come off it. There's a candle flickers any animal's silhouette on cathedral walls, so why am I the mammal the village idiot's always eyeing? Jet fuel spills low-totem over the things I'd rather keep theoretical. It's the air's there to attest to a wing's agency. Two conditions meet, molding the aim of the coming age, which I'd spell out if I weren't inadvertently anti-sage.

real speech Out in which as an act were house to
definition

S CULPTURE SEEKS articulation of the air around it. Thus, a heron thrusting overhead mutes modernism. It was my hope to build an ethics of the animal with no auditory equivalent, to occupy the puppeteer's right hand, insist on dusk as the sole verb to pulsate a mosquito into action. A pox on the precision with which one renders the meticulous details required for an etching of anything is acquiescence to photography's fossilization of the digital age. If entropy is inherent to all imagery, I resemble nothing so much as a sentence hacked out of speech, a reproduction of the ax within reach.

a novel of human noise

delinquent agency

•

•

CONSIDERING THE FIRST AXIOM of Machiavellian action, what strikes me is usually something blunt. Can one get more redundant than a digital fiction's novel sense of ethics? Let someone else overcome the posthuman megalopolis of micro-data makes a lexical noise the delinquent exuberance in which these waning thoughts find agency. It's not like a body of work can up and walk away. Forget the psychosociolinguistic phenomenon. Let's return to transcribing our seams, fusing the difference between method and doctrine in an anodyne for the new consciousness, where the reason metaphysics abuts philosophy remains beyond me.

to animal to hand into detail is to fossil speech

WHEN SUBJECT TO a conspicuous lack of location, one need only climb a real tree to see the artifice rooted in the external world. This is an assertion of descriptive speech. Out of ambiguity comes a sentence in which the office building acts as verb, in which an imaginative act of architecture pushed aside the story one fell into as though it were a bed in one's own house and not the culmination of another's attention to particulars. Perhaps the camera is unreliable. Perhaps unreliability is the locus of representation. Think of it as a working definition for neighborhood, the opposite of being elsewhere, a branch of remoteness becoming an unuttered address.

•

•

or by Here for any so keep aim of which if

I F THE FUNCTION OF THE CAMERA is to explain itself to the operator. If the page on which the wall appears does not allow for the casting of a shadow. If the shadow is absent from the photograph. If absence is operative. If the explanation of an envelope to a balcony is not an order. If one were to describe the mechanics of longing as a desire for oil. If an oblique reference to photosynthesis fills the screen. If the wobbly dirge meets the elongated fugue. If sound is manipulated. If manipulation elicits the sculpted noise of its self-portrait. If this is a picture. If the primary function of representation is thwarted. If the operation is contorted.

speaking inclusive renders a process ghost As of
    another

A BIOCHEMICAL REACTION bakes bread. From here to there through prepositions. To go by way of that which already moves one gives a visible thought sayable being. This is the sort of English up with which I cannot put. Orbiting parataxis metropolis, just about the most fun a neo-flaneur can hope for. Meanwhile, an entirely different motif jettisons its high-horse scrutiny for a donkey's silhouette. Outcroppings are similarly elevated. One packs in what one can, as the real point of art is a subtle reiteration of the is, ain't it? The way I see it, we're all partially tainted.

one and one

one both out of its ambivalence from Two
one and one In order

example

TIN GLINTS off the kind of lintel holds a pro-
crastinated thought this far from its frame.
The machine in me moves, makes a case for eras-
ing space. An ancestral insistence? No, I think in
sloping frames, far from the famished complexity
gives an ode its self-effacing order. An odd creaking
cuts through ten feet of floorboard, keeps sleep an
awareness of itself, mints my hope to yesterday's
anonymity—an art to affirm the dull subsistence
subjectivity's flung into the context masher. I'm
nothing if not practical. Submit to necessity and
you've built a home; live there and you're evicted
from the metronome.

that one

as though description everywhere. All

CRAMMING SYLLABLES into a canopy of trees elevates one above the hillside. A lofty idea of creation hovers there. I suppose an admission of absolute freedom, pulverize the supposition into a fine powder, adding one part perceptive integrity for every three concrete images of the divine. As an idea adheres to its neighbor, a crowd discards its propriety. How else to put it? Between the house of realist fiction and a reel of film depicting someone reading, the poem is a sort of alleyway of experience, a missing equation chalked on the blackboard destroyed by its own negation.

the attempt instead of instead of under likeness

as to appear neither offering

•

•

O N SECOND THOUGHT is a sorry way to start catching wind in one's sail. Nautical! Now we're getting somewhere. There's a certain *je ne sais quoi* to it, as though the word were undulating toward its definition. Although I'm afraid this, as well, is a dead end. Like a simile pushed through a cul-de-sac a sweep of cars shares with the shoreline the convex sound of a thing caving in. On second thought, let's erase the road. I'm hoping for more specifics here, an innocuous distraction that might offer a spotlight to that serrated leaf, explaining the appearance of its shadow underneath.

of analogy
How abstract

of the picture
Were it a system

THAT WHEN ASCRIBED TO traditional tech-
niques for introducing motifs a terra-cotta
levity defines the decorative arts as a scarcity of
good building stone erecting a sudden excursion
into grotesque erudition is already widely known.
What's not is the role classic doctrine plays in pot-
tery fragments the life of the new state's packed
into its explanation for imperialist antiquity. It's
cast as the fledgling mammal meant to elicit a
rush of applause whenever it appears to dissolve
into vapor. In order to fully illustrate the conceit,
our narrator suggests drawing a mastodon without
lifting your pen from the paper.

around admitting disposition music and whatever
adding

IMPETUOUS categorical imperative? A bed of rotting pine needles? Both sink a simile in me, extending the lesson a story of little consequence broils to brown the underside of an indigestible moral. A sudden accumulation of clouds in the shape of something slightly angelic or the sentence over which they've gathered? Time does its two-step between punctuating. Clouds part. See that ray of light landing on the side of the house next door? Illuminating prose is an awfully iridescent pose, so I color the word *ocular* with mine eyes closed.

the screen is perfect

Thus, actors

the screen has

no thought of excess

•

•

A ND YET, perhaps it is among the wavering
bits of music, the clang of percussion cutting
through any discernible melody, that rays of light
bend the whole of landscape in some nameless seed
growing over the course of several millennia into
the hardened stuff of history, as one must, after
all, master microscope as well as telescope, note as
well as chord, the dynamics of solvency and subtle
exchanges of the plant kingdom, in order to see not
only the square mesh in front of one's face but also
the slant of the hills just beyond the screen door,
the exterior's décor.

in this need moves a line
A second
experience

WIND SMACKS the windshield. Maybe it's the other way around. A single beat's an oxymoron. Is this degenerating into a dull accumulation of minor defeats? I mean insect sheets, how they force syncopation from the wipers' standard time. Accordingly, one must advance to sustain interest. Who says economics lacks a narrative hook? I'm passing an accident out of necessity, an eighteen-wheeler out of fear, a water tower sitting atop roadside pines simply for its looks.

those points
its vestige
its place

EVEN NOW the century advances toward you its pseudo-romantic indoctrination to the denouement a Sunday drive makes of one's fatalistic sense of destination. Cherry Creek Road is, of course, composed of concrete, another neorealist line on the abstract canvas of the earth. The Decorator Extends Her Arm Upward? The Underside of a Praying Mantis as Seen Through a Pane of Frosted Glass? No, I'd prefer for my titles a world free of affect, as one unknowingly stumbles onto the perfect stage by attributing captions to an otherwise blank page.

keep the theater in vantage point by metaphor
if something

for better

•

•

D ON'T EXPECT any fireworks here. This is a paragraph about uprooting ornamentation in the way of perceiving the world, an argument for moving prose privileging a shifting position on the surface of the earth. It takes as its percussive beat the presence of a mocking bird unimpeachably outside my bedroom window. Nature's encroachment springs its central aphorism. I find myself at an impasse, get around it by installing a clump of chrysanthemums in the center of the room I've yet to delineate. A wall's a wall. One looks both ways from a window. There's no social power in the terminal cluster that ends a flower.

light
then
thought's course again arranged
the same which with its surplus

M Y TRAGIC FLAW is a tertiary comeback, lol-lygagging its way into the fraction of self-erasure one's facial muscles produce prior to a bout of all-out laughter. From this high window, the trees seem as comical as they do ordained with the common airs of solemnity we'd so often grant them. Little to speak of lifts up to its exception, mulching music by stretching a ritualistic listen to its thinnest point. Tinniest joint? What's a good ear anyhow? Underneath, notes deteriorate. Rocks in a grove clocks in as perfect landscape fodder, a commandeered salute. The table's there for putting things on. The tower's there. The gunner's gone.

in which Sun as a marker makes the background
of analogy an instruction

•

•

I'D LIKE TO MIME THE SUBPLOT of the last film I saw, although, as it constitutes an undercurrent whose subtlety is such that the ripples now appearing on the surface might be mistaken for a momentary change in wind velocity or the wake of a passing motorboat, I'm afraid the movement would entail nothing more than an intermittent tapping of my left pinkie on these newly pressed slacks. Where an ocean of thought's an underwater ideal, woe is everyone trying to walk there.

giving an inch

How else to cover logic

Such are the comings and goings, the scant words of greeting or departure rolled off the tongue so often now that their intimacy with one's own body is manifest as something greater than the escape of an audible vocalization, a near physical gesture, widening the aperture with which one had sensed the air around one to weaken, drifting toward the atmosphere of some far-off planet whose ecosystem is unable to sustain our definition of life: a kind of eventual collapsing into oneself, where to lay claim to the few square feet of terra firma a refocusing of the lens had brought is to mollify the ground upon which we're indelibly caught.

is ambiguity expression
is intention use
Why

•

•

THE FIRST OPTION is to rattle the world in its frame. The second frames the world in its rattle. Between them, an amplifier without its instrument. This is not a metaphor. Each paragraph requires the participants to reposition themselves. From up here, I can make out the action as if it were taking space. Several ants beelining back to headquarters. Reportage lacks ideology as painting lacks performance. Some of these statements are false, including the present example. If one were to take transgression as one's starting point, then it would be limitation that throws one satisfyingly out of joint.

to one it is into one to one yes listening to it

an other

•

•

To go on recording with deceptive simplicity who's who in the wood-grain faces of one's piano animal. A great deal of emotional identification on the part of the audience is lost. For want of what? The chorus acting too uppity? Call it injecting a flute trio for the letting loose of birds with a few meaningless measures of music. The resulting sound's terrible monotony trues a modern ear, mistakes otherworldliness for arrogance, orchestral expression for a set of footprints leading away from the scorched university—the studious avoidance of any progression suggesting a chord or key.

describe as image as subject to intension then say

THE PITFALLS of inadequate definition dust off their outmoded fashion magazines. Is speech a platform for lecturing one's self a solid foundation? The window looks like the door. The ceiling looks like the door. The door looks like the door. A parcel's more mysterious than a package, though both are bound to anticipation's delivery of a stalled present, a slight incline in thinking time. A few strokes and an awful looking island emerges. When no one's listening, these arbitrary assumptions know it's okay to disappear, an image irrelevant to prose, inside of which meaning comes to a close.

anything on show is of the theory of
entire returns, a model expressed

•

•

Let's get physical. So this is what it feels like to run a trademarked frame of reference up the flagpole and hope for the impending invasion to elicit a postrevolutionary lean on repeat listen. Icons are abrasive because they're so easy to ignore. A pair of docks, water on the rocks. The afternoon peals away and I'm stuck cleaning tread marks from a perfectly functional book. Forget physical; let's get embryonic. For example, the objects in the room aren't doing anything objectionable, sitting in their assigned space, but here I am, veering toward rhetorical extremes by assigning each a human face.

is one is which on one's way is for whomever

THE WIND mills around an Afro-Cuban idiom. Click. Clock. This machine's sole purpose is to ensure the applecart remains upright. If you'd like to pet a llama, insert one into the paragraph. Thus began our thesis on mimesis. Cloud banks. Riverbanks. Regular banks with money in them! A tacky advertisement for the army morphs into a mountainside view. My advice, invest in assurance. Relief, mapping its lipstick marks on the butt end of a burning cigarette, says tame me, calls this the new pastoral tranquillity.

of what useless desire to value detail the instance
as is

•

•

I BEGIN by implicit contradiction to allow shiny horses galloping in tandem through the center of a recently abandoned painting. This is outright expression. What begins with few brushstrokes ends as turpentine muscles the rest of the free radicals from their folding-chair moralism. Smell's only an amorphous solution of what one swallows. Don't get me started with those crickets kicking on. Stumbling out of the epiphany stockade, night makes a sober metaphor. The first symptom of motion picture sickness: being content to stare at whatever's there.

to catch to make again until action

I N THE PROJECTION of time's porcelain-like consistency, simultaneously hardened and delicate, smooth though nearly glistening, as though it were a form of water oscillating forever between the solidity of ice and the infinitesimal degree of temperature just above freezing, there comes a definitive, nearly palpable moment, one suddenly wrenched from the metronome—now ticking experience, now, memory—that allows little more than a trivial run of scales or minor derivation from the theme to arise, dance around a bit until the tether, fully taut, reminds one at last replicating the clock's an impossible task.

as a formula occurs in narrative

So THIS is where Salt river runneth over, between the immaculate image of one's ideal machine and a couple of phrases praising the efficacy of leaving well enough alone. First, a doomsday device. Later, a lesson in vice. What this lever does is irrelevant, I'd rather covet the longbow some violence with the vernacular draws to take the bark off our fish-tank benevolence. It's a lofty ambition equates its own face with the abovementioned image. Just beneath the bulldozer, a spot offers the exact amount of shade I'd need to relax. It takes resiliency to stretch the facts.

comment to pass on question is a picture
    remaining

R EPUTATION OUTREACH? Recent studies having shown the new royal we needs a leavening agent to loosen pre-nostalgia, its still, uphill gardening. It's still uphill gardening. A swell of bird noise from the ivy? Conceptual space? A thought caught in the din leaves me before there's time to trace it back to a for-your-own-good nudge from the nest. This is music discomposed. Take note, audience is an arguably unclear concept. Take note, half an octave higher. Listen, a concave vireo tangled in the time signature rounds out the composition.

from a bouquet of place—articulation
and labor's sound of primacy